Doppelgänger

A Tragicomic Novella by D. L. Lewis

PUBLISHER'S NOTE

The following story is fictional and does not depict
any actual person or event.

NOVELS BY D. L. LEWIS

Where Wolves Talk

Something in the House: California Gothic

Copyright © D. L. Lewis 2014

All rights reserved. No part of this book may be reproduced or transmitted in any form or by any means, electronic or mechanical, including photocopying, recording, or by any information storage and retrieval system without the written permission of the author.

Front Cover Image from a drawing by D. L. Lewis © 2014 D. L. Lewis

Picture of Basset Hound in Chapter Two heading and on back cover from a photograph by Bonnie van den Born, http://www.bonfoto.nl

Picture of woman's head in Chapter One heading from a drawing by Leonardo da Vinci

Dedicated to the late great Peter Falk

> You may charge me with murder—or want of sense—
> (We are all of us weak at times):
> But the slightest approach to a false pretense
> Was never among my crimes!
>
> *Lewis Carroll*

Table of Contents

Chapter One - Page 1

Chapter Two - Page 29

Author's Statement

I had some unusual experiences a while ago which inspired me to write this story. I shall detail them here, and allow you to draw whatever conclusion you like best.

Earlier this year, I went into a store near my home to buy a few things. When I got to the cash register, the cashier looked at me in surprise and said, "You were just here!" I told her I was not just there; I hadn't been in that store for weeks. She insisted I had been at her cash register just a few minutes earlier. I suggested it was someone who looked like me. She told me the woman was wearing exactly the same clothes I was wearing.

A few months later, I went back to the same store. When I got to the cash register, the cashier (a different lady) said, "You're back already?" It was the same as the previous incident, except when I told the cashier this had happened to me before, she asked me, "Was that woman (the previous double) buying the same things you were buying?" I told her I didn't know. The cashier looked into my shopping cart and told me the double who had preceded me that day was buying the same things as me: four bags of bird seed.

Both of these cashiers were sincere women who were as perplexed and discomfited by the situation as was I. The easy explanation would be that they were both lying, but I assure you, that was not the case.

D. L. Lewis

 # Chapter 1

Location: rural Kenwood in Sonoma County, California.
Time: late autumn, 2014.
Dwellings: older houses; nothing fancy.

SATURDAY AFTERNOON

Emma stood in the open doorway of the house; her eyes wide as she stared at the visitor who had just rung the bell. "What's wrong?" Leah asked.

Emma put one hand over her mouth; unable to speak.

"You're not going to invite me inside?"

A few incoherent words were mumbled under the hand in response to the query.

"What did you say?"

The hand was dropped. "You're already here!"

"Oh . . . I see." Leah nodded. "Sorry 'bout that."

"What's going on?"

"Can I come inside, please? It's cold out here."

Emma backed away two steps and allowed her visitor to enter.

"Let me get that." Leah pried her friend's hand away from the brass knob she was clutching in a near death-grip and closed the door.

Emma looked . . . well; imagine someone who's just seen a ghost. You know the routine: mouth open, eyes bugging out, muscles rigid. If she'd been a cartoon character, her short black hair would've been standing straight out from her head like the quills of an agitated porcupine.

"I can explain," Leah said.

Emma continued to stare at her visitor.

"I'm not really here already."

"Yes, you are! You're in the front room sitting on my couch!"

"No! That's not me; I mean, it's not exactly me."

Emma closed her eyes and took a deep breath.

"Really . . . it's not me. It's not even real. Come on." Leah walked from the foyer and into the living room. She pointed at the empty couch. "See?"

Emma looked at the vacant sofa and shook her head. "I must be losing my mind."

"It's not you. I've got a *doppelgänger*."

"A what?"

"A doppelgänger: a double-goer. Well, actually, a better word for it is *vardøger*, which I'm sure I'm pronouncing wrong. That's the Norwegian name for a sort of spirit predecessor: a ghostly double that precedes a person and performs their actions in advance."

"I had a ghost sitting on my couch?"

"It's not really a ghost. No one knows for sure exactly what it is. It's just one of those unexplainable things that happen, you know?"

"I don't know."

"Did it talk to you?"

"No. I answered the door, said hello, and asked why you were dressed in a costume and you, I mean it, just walked in and sat on the couch without saying a word. As soon as it sat down, you rang the doorbell."

"A costume?"

"It was wearing something that looked like a fancy nightgown and you, it, had a white silk scarf over its head held in place by a flowered headpiece and you, it, was wearing a bunch of pearl necklaces."

"That's the way I'm dressed in a self-portrait I drew a couple of years ago."

"Does the thing always show up dressed like that?"

"No. Maybe it did that because I was looking at the portrait before I left today. It usually wears what I'm wearing when I leave my house, though."

"Does this happen a lot?"

"No, and I'm glad for that. It upsets me. I used to waste time trying to find a rational explanation for how I could be someplace before I got there, and of course there's no explanation. There are theories out there about doppelgängers being caused by quantum time shifts or epilepsy, but that's just stuff made up by scientists trying to explain away something they don't want to believe in."

"Epilepsy?" Emma took a chair while Leah settled onto the couch.

"Yeah. It's ridiculous. I don't have epilepsy, and even if I did, how could my brain function, or malfunction, cause other people to see my exact twin arrive at my destination a few minutes before me? I swear; the things scientists will do and say in order to continue their funding is amazing. Their patrons are really scared of the possibility of supernatural phenomena being real, don't you think?"

Emma chuckled. "They better not study you, then! With your premonitions and whatnot, you'd terrify 'em."

"Yeah. It's a comfort knowing the double-goer thing happens to other people often enough that there are quite a few personal stories out there on the web. The first time the thing showed up, I didn't know it happened to other people, and it really upset me, till I researched it and found it's been happening to other people for a long time. Still; it knocks me for a loop every time it happens."

"Why didn't you tell me about this before?"

"I never tell anyone about it till they've seen it for themselves. It's hard to believe if you haven't seen it."

"I understand that."

"I can't remember why I came here."

"You are rattled, aren't you?"

"Yup."

"You came here to get my old wok."

"Right! You're sure you don't need it anymore?"

"I'm sure. I don't like having to deal with cleaning the cast iron. I prefer my new stainless-steel one."

"Thanks."

"It's in the kitchen, on the counter next to the oven."

"I'll be going now. I've got groceries in my car, and I was at my jitterbug class before I went shopping. I need a shower! I'll just grab that wok and be on my way."

"See ya later."

Leah parked her car in the garage and carried bags of groceries into the kitchen. As she set the last bag on the counter, she felt something soft brush against her lower leg. Looking down, she saw Malcolm the Destroyer—a huge cat with long ivory hair, four white paws, and dark Siamese markings—striding past. He turned, sat down, and looked up at her with his blue eyes. "You want treats, handsome?" She pulled a small foil pouch from one of the grocery bags, tore it open, and set a handful of crunchy tidbits on the floor before him. The sound of the pouch being opened brought three more creatures into the kitchen: Priscilla and Tallulah—both long-haired tortoiseshell tabbies—and Felix the Cat: a shorthaired black and white fellow with hefty tomcat cheeks and no tail.

Though full-grown, Priscilla had the angelic face of a kitten, with big innocent eyes that made her appear harmless and sweet. Felix fell for that face every time he saw it, and he walked forward to give her a gentle sniff-kiss on her nose.

A string of loud curses comprehensible only to cats erupted from Priscilla as she slapped Felix hard on one cheek. He backed away; head lowered in shame.

"You never learn, Felix." Leah stroked his head as he purred. This boy bounced back quick from every insult hurled upon him; probably as a result of the hard life he lived as a semi-feral stray before he was made into a pampered house cat.

The lady dispensed treats to the three new arrivals and began to put away her groceries. As she passed the sliding-glass door that opened onto the yard behind her house, she noticed a red hen on the door mat staring into the kitchen. There were a few drops of water beaded up on her back feathers: a light rain had started to fall.

"Want to come in early, do you?" Leah opened the door, and the chicken entered. She promptly pooped on the linoleum floor, and the lady cleaned it up with a paper towel and spray cleaner.

Felix saw the hen and just couldn't resist. He walked towards her; a predatory air in his steps. "No, Felix!"

The warning was ignored. Felix got within three feet of the chicken before she charged: a scarlet-feathered bull going for the red cape that was the tomcat. The cat saw the fearless resolve in the bird's eyes, spun around, and ran from the room.

The hen sauntered over to a tall louvered door. "Okay, Chicken Little; bedtime for you." Leah opened the door and the bird went inside. The lady had turned her pantry into a warm night-time sanctuary for the chicken, with a thick layer of clean straw covering the floor. She refreshed the water dish and put a cob of corn on the bedding. It had to be organic corn, as Chicken Little refused to eat corn bearing the scent of agricultural poisons.

Leah closed the door. The hen would burrow down in the straw and sleep till the dawn light coming through the pantry window awakened her.

She finished putting away her groceries and went into the shower stall for a quick suds and rinse. After drying off, she took a packaged salad from the fridge and headed for her home office. Standing before her computer, she put on her headphones, opened her iTunes library, and clicked on the song "Mannish Boy" by Muddy Waters. As the music entered her ears, her hips began to move. She danced around the room, letting out occasional whoops of music-inspired joy, until the song ended.

She switched to a classical-music radio station and sat down before her desktop. Opening a graphics application, she began importing images and text for an ad she was composing. It was a tedious and unpleasant task, but the hours she would spend slaving over promotional material for a bank would wear her out and guarantee a sound night's sleep.

SUNDAY MORNING

The nightmare was pure horrible chaos: dark, garbled images churning in confusion; feelings of anger, pain, and death.

Leah broke out of the dream and sat up, gasping and trembling all over. "Emma's dead!" She knew it without a doubt: her friend had just died.

She jumped out of bed and dashed to her closet. Pulling out a pair of old cowboy boots, she put them on and stuffed the legs of her pajamas inside the leather shafts.

Chicken Little's morning calls could be heard: the morning sun was shining into the pantry window. Leah ran to the kitchen and released the bird into the yard. Her keys and cell phone were sitting on the table, and she grabbed them and stuffed them into the breast pocket of her pajama top. Running to the front door, she pulled a coat from the rack next to it, put it on, and ran back to the kitchen, where a door led into the garage. She jumped into her car and took off.

Emma's house was less than a mile down the country road. Leah parked in the driveway and ran to the front door. She rang the bell over and over; intermittently pounding on the aged wood of the door. She knew no one would answer, but felt she had to do it anyway.

"This is stupid!" She ran to the side of the house and opened the iron-barred gate that led to the backyard. "I know where she is," the woman whispered. She raced to the two sliding-glass doors that gave a view into the dining room and saw Emma lying on the floor. One of the glass doors was open, the other one had been broken, and there were patches on the hardwood floor that looked like smeared prints from muddy shoes. The same prints were distributed in a trail across the patio; turning into muddy holes tracking through the grass of the wild backyard.

Leah tried to stop the hyperventilation that was overtaking her. She retrieved her cell phone from its pocket and called 911. "My friend is dead!" she shouted. She recited the address and put the phone away.

She looked through the doors at the body, and wanted to get far away from it. Running around the house to the front, she sat on the porch steps and waited.

She could hear the sound of a siren in the distance. A few seconds later, an ambulance pulled up in front of the house. Leah led the EMTs to the open door in the back and returned to the front porch. A few minutes later, a police car arrived, followed by two more. Four officers emerged from the vehicles, and three of them followed Leah's gestures indicating they should go to the back of the building.

One officer approached Leah and looked her over. Her long dark-blonde hair hadn't been brushed since she went to bed the night before and was a mess. The ill-matched ensemble of striped blue pajamas, red cowboy boots, and green trench coat enhanced the oddity of her appearance. "What's going on?" the officer asked.

"She's dead."
"What happened?"
"I don't know."
"Do you live here?"
"No."
"Why are you here?"
"I, uh . . . I had a bad dream, and I came here to see if she was okay. I pounded on the door and rang the bell over and over, and when she didn't answer, I went around back and saw her lying there. I didn't go inside."

"If you didn't go inside, how do you know she's dead? She could be unconscious."

"Sometimes I just know things."
"She's a friend of yours?"
"Yes."
"Do you have some ID?"
"No."

The officer's green eyes narrowed. "No ID?"

"I was in a hurry. I grabbed my keys and phone and came here. I'm sorry. I left it at home."

"That's your car in the driveway?"
"Yeah."
"Any registration in there?"
"Yeah; it's in my glovebox. I'll get it."

The officer followed her to the passenger side of the sedan. She unlocked the door, found the slip of paper, and handed it to him. "Is this your current address?"

"Yes. It's less than a mile down the road."

"I'll follow you there so you can show me your ID." He activated a device plugged into one ear and talked with an unseen party as he walked towards his patrol car. "You shouldn't be driving without a license, you know."

"I know. I'm sorry."

When they arrived at her home, Leah showed him her driver's license. He conveyed the information to his invisible colleague and; after learning she had no warrants, etc.; said to her, "Stay here. Someone will be along to question you shortly." He left.

Leah fed Chicken Little and the cats, then flopped down on the couch; still wearing her trench coat and boots. She laid there, not moving, for an hour and a half before the doorbell rang. She couldn't feel any emotions at all, and wondered why.

She rose and opened the door. A black-haired man of middle age wearing a rumpled tan raincoat over a grey business suit stood there, holding a black wallet in one hand. He broke into a goofy grin, let the wallet fall open, and showed his badge. "Morning, Miss. I'm Lieutenant Pietro; Homicide."

"Come in."

He followed her into the living room and looked around; eyeballing every detail of the place. The room was pleasant, but a bit untidy. The furnishings were unremarkable except for one piece: a single-seat bench with curved arms ending in carvings like those seen on the prows of ancient Viking warships. "Interesting bench," the detective said.

"That's a reproduction of a Norwegian king's throne. My people are descended from Vikings."

"Do you live alone here?"

"Yes."

The detective's head jerked back in surprise as Malcolm the Destroyer shot out from under a low table and flew past him, heading for refuge elsewhere in the house. "You have a cat."

"Yes."

"My wife loves cats. Me; I like dogs. I get along with 'em, ya know? My wife keeps tellin' me cats are easier to take care of; they wash themselves, ya know; but me, I like my dog. When he starts to smell bad, I throw him in the tub and lather him up."

"You throw him in the tub?"

"Well, I kinda set him in there real gentle. It's hard to throw a seventy-pound basset hound."

"Uh, huh."

"How many cats do you have, Miss?"

"A few."

"Do you let them go outside?"

"No. Only my chicken goes outside, and she always comes in before nightfall so the wildlife won't eat her."

"You let a chicken come in the house?"

"Yes."

"Well! Ain't that unusual?"

12

"I suppose it is."

"Me; I wouldn't let a chicken come in the house. They poop all over, don't they?"

"I deal with it."

"How?"

"What do pets have to do with my dead friend?"

"Sorry, Miss. Can we sit down?"

"Yes."

He sank into the cushions of the sofa and Leah took a chair. "Nice couch; real comfortable."

"I bought it used on Craigslist."

The detective nodded. "How well did you know Miss MacIntyre?"

"Very well. We've been friends for a few years now. We have lunch together pretty often, and talk on the phone at least once a week."

"How did she make a living?"

"She invented and produces a water-purification system. I guess I should say, 'produced.' It's going to be a while before I can accept the fact that she's now a person who exists in the past tense."

"What do you do for a living?"

"I'm a graphic designer."

"I see." He pulled a small pad of paper from a pocket inside his raincoat.

"Are you going to ask me for a pencil?"

The man smiled "You're onto me, aren't you?"

"I bet you've got a cigar on you somewhere."

"I do."

"We all have our little eccentricities, Lieutenant Columbo. I'll get you a pencil if you'll wait a moment."

She went into the kitchen and returned with the writing implement.

His smile vanished as she handed him the pencil. He squinted and rubbed his forehead with the tips of his fingers. "We have a little problem with your story."

"Yes?"

"You said you didn't go inside the house."

"That's right."

"There's a surveillance camera at the front of Miss MacIntyre's house that feeds to her computer. We looked at the images from this morning, and it shows you going into her house."

"That's impossible."

"The camera doesn't lie. It shows you going onto her front porch. A few minutes later, you go onto her front porch again and about thirty seconds later, you leave the front porch and run in the direction of the side gate to the back of the house."

"Does the camera show me going through the front door and into the house?"

"The walls of the porch hide the front door from the camera. Since the only way you could get off the porch without being in view of the camera is to go through the front door, we must conclude that you went into the house."

"I swear I did not!"

The detective scribbled away at his pad of paper.

"I want to see that video!"

"What good will that do?"

"Listen . . . you're calling me a liar, and I know I'm not. Let me prove it!"

14

"There's nothing you can say that will disprove the evidence of the video."

"I know there is; I know it!"

"How do you know?"

"The same way I know that when you go out to your car, it'll refuse to start. Nothing will happen when you turn the key. It'll start when you put it into drive gear."

"That's ridiculous. You can't start an automatic transmission in drive!"

"My freedom is on the line here. Please, go out there and try to start your car."

"I'll do it only to prove to you that you're crazy."

"That would make two of us, Lieutenant Columbo."

"You're coming with me."

They went outside to the car: a beat-up blue Citröen hatchback. "Couldn't find yourself an old Peugeot convertible, I guess."

"Get in!"

Leah got into the passenger seat as the detective went around to the driver's side. Sitting down, he put his key in the ignition and turned it. The result was dead silence. He tried again: silence. He took his hand away from the key, crossed his arms over his chest, and glared at the steering wheel.

"Afraid to be proven wrong, Lieutenant?"

He put one foot on the brake, shifted into drive, turned the key, and winced as the engine turned over.

"Gonna let me see that video now, copper?"

The lieutenant seated himself before Emma's computer and began to click on various windows. "Here it is."

Leah stood behind him, watching over his shoulder. She saw herself walk onto the front porch, and watched as she approached the porch a second time. Something was missing from the first version of herself; it took her a few seconds to realize what it was. "Lieutenant—can you run it again? I see something."

"All right."

"Look!"

"What is it?"

"Do you see the shadows? Everything's casting a shadow, right?"

"Yes."

"Everything but that image of what's supposed to be me."

The detective put his face closer to the screen. "You're right."

"Now watch as I go onto the porch the second time. I'm casting shadows, see?"

"Yes." He played the clip over three times. "Someone must have altered the file somehow."

Leah pulled up a chair and sat down. "It takes time to manipulate a video file. There was no time. Emma's body was still warm when the EMTs arrived, wasn't it?"

"Yes."

"I think I know why there are no shadows, but if I tell you, you won't believe me."

"Miss . . . you should probably refrain from giving me a theoretical explanation. The lack of shadows brings the integrity of the video into question. You made your point. Just accept your victory and be on your way. I'll get an officer to drive you home."

"Okay."

"Just one more thing . . ."

"What?"

"Don't leave town, Miss."

Pietro watched the video over and over. Was it some kind of electronic hiccup that caused the repeating of the woman's actions? The movements were identical; he could see that. He ran the two segments side by side in separate windows: the steps and arm movements of the shadowless first appearance were a perfect match to the second one. He could see, though, that the breeze-driven actions of fallen leaves and the tree branches at the edge of the frame were not identical, and neither was the motion of the lady's hair as it stirred in the wind.

This did not make sense, and if there was anything Pietro hated, it was nonsense. He got into his car, which had gone back to starting in a proper manner, and drove to the woman's home.

Leah had gone back to lying on the couch as soon as she got back to her house. She'd kicked off her boots, but still wore her pajamas and coat. When the sound of the front bell chimed through the room, she rose and went to the door. "Lieutenant."

"Sorry to bother you, Miss. I wonder if you can help me with something."

"Of course. Come in and have a seat." Leah fell into a chair and put her bare feet up on the coffee table.

"Aren't your feet cold?"

"Yes, but I don't have enough ambition to go get a pair of socks out of a drawer. I'll live with it."

The detective saw a piled-up afghan on the end of the sofa. He picked it up and covered the woman's feet.

"Thank you."

"You might want to try combing your hair sometime soon. Good grooming is essential for a positive attitude." Pietro pulled a pencil from a pocket inside his coat before seating himself on the couch. "I forgot to return this to you." He set it on the coffee table.

"Thanks. So what is it you need help with?"

"I've been looking at the video, and so have my tech guys. We can't come up with any answers."

"I'm sure you can't."

"You said you might have a theory that would explain it."

"Okay—you asked for it." Leah put her feet on the floor and sat upright. She arranged the blanket over her legs. "I've got a doppelgänger."

"Really."

"You know what that is?"

"Yes, I've heard the word before."

"I call it a doppelgänger 'cause it's a more commonly known word. It's actually a vardøger: a double that precedes me and carries out my actions in advance. It's kind of like a guardian spirit."

"Uh, huh."

Leah had a sudden thought. "I can prove it!"

"I doubt that very much."

"Did you view the surveillance video from yesterday?"

"We went back as far as around eleven last night. We'll see more as the investigation proceeds."

"I visited Emma yesterday afternoon. She told me the vardøger got there just before me, and it was dressed in a kind of costume."

"Uh, huh."

"I'll show you. Hang on a minute." Leah trotted into her bedroom, picked up a framed picture that was leaning against one wall, and returned to the living room. "This is what it was wearing." She held up the pencil drawing.

"Did you draw that?"

"Yes."

"Nice work. You should be famous."

"Fine art doesn't pay the mortgage, so I don't do it anymore."

"That's a shame."

"This is what you'll see on the video. Emma said it got there just before me. There's no way I could've gone inside wearing that, changed into street clothes, and gotten back to the front door again in what was probably less than two minutes. And I expect you'll see the thing isn't casting a shadow, just like you saw already."

"You don't have a twin sister?"

"No, I don't! Even if I did, she'd be casting shadows, wouldn't she?"

"I suppose so."

"Until this morning, I didn't think the thing was visible to a camera. That's interesting."

"It's interesting to you, maybe. To me, it's just irritating."

"Sorry."

"I'll look at the video, but even if it shows what you say it will, I'm going to have a hard time believing your explanation."

"I can't wait to hear what your logical explanation for it will be, Lieutenant."

"We'll come up with something, Miss."

"I'm sure you saw all the big muddy footprints on the floor and patio, and the tracks in the grass. It's obvious I wasn't the only person at the house that morning. My feet aren't that big!"

"Those tracks lead to . . . never mind."

"Any DNA evidence or fingerprints?"

"None yet on the body or in the dining room, except for the victim's prints, of course. We're still working on the crime scene."

"You might find some of my hairs in the living room from my visit yesterday, and my fingerprints should be on the inside front doorknob."

"Let's assume for a moment you aren't an accomplice to the murder. Do you know of anyone who might have a reason to kill her?"

"No. She was a wonderful person; no enemies. She managed to be successful in her line of work without stepping on anyone's toes."

"Did she have any romantic attachments?"

"No. That's one of the things we had in common: we both feel, or felt, that romance isn't worth the trouble it usually causes. And like me, she's never been married."

"What about family?"

"Her parents live on the East Coast; I don't know exactly where. She was an only child, like me."

"It's possible the killer was after something in the house, and was scared off by the noise you made pounding on the front door and ringing the bell."

"He would've been scared off by the vardøger who got there before me."

"Uh, huh. We haven't seen any signs of the intruder going anywhere in the house except the dining room. I noticed she has several pieces of art on display. Do you know if any of them are valuable? If we knew what the killer was after, that might provide some leads."

"Let me think." Leah was feeling very tired. She closed her eyes.

"Take your time."

She opened her eyes. "Emma bought all her pieces from local artists. None of them are famous yet. I can't imagine someone killing so they could steal the work of unknown artists. It'd be hard to sell, and even if they could sell it, they couldn't get much for it. As far as I know, the only things in the house that would be attractive to a thief are her computer and cell phone. She didn't wear expensive jewelry, and never seemed to have any cash on hand."

Pietro pulled out his pad, took the pencil from the coffee table, and scribbled a few quick notes. "You haven't asked me how she was killed."

"Would you tell me if I asked?"

"No."

"That's what I thought." Leah knew her friend had been shot in the heart, but she wasn't about to incriminate herself by exposing knowledge acquired through psychic means.

"So far, Miss Thorsen, you're the only person with a motive."

"Motive? I don't have a motive!"

"Yes, you do. We found a copy of her will on her computer, and you're the sole beneficiary."

"What?"

"Are you saying you didn't know about that?"

"Yes!" Leah felt sick. "Why would she leave everything to me? What about her parents?"

"All we know is what the will says, and it says everything—her money, her business, and her house with all its contents—goes to you."

She covered her face with both hands. "Oh, no."

Pietro scribbled a few more notes on his pad. "Right now, all we have against you is motive and opportunity. That's not enough to convict, so it's not enough to charge you."

Leah nodded.

"We've looked into your finances. You have a lot of money in savings, a steady income, and no debts other than your mortgage. You paid a thousand dollars in vet bills when your chicken had a leg problem. It appears that you're a compassionate person who isn't desperate for cash. That profile won't save you if evidence against you comes up, of course."

She nodded again.

"We'd like you to come by the crime scene tomorrow. Can you do that for us?"

"Yeah."

"Is ten in the morning good for you?"

"Yeah."

"I'll be going now. Don't forget to bring your hen inside before it gets dark."

MONDAY MORNING

Leah was at Emma's house right on time. She'd managed to comb her hair and put on fresh clothing: a navy sweatsuit and running shoes.

Pietro was waiting for her on the front porch. "Good morning, Miss Thorsen. Would you come with me?" She followed him to the back of the house. When they reached the dining-room doors, she started to tremble. "Please explain exactly what you saw and did here."

She did as he asked. Getting the words out was difficult; her voice was shaking. "Come inside, please."

She walked into the dining room and stood near the tape outline showing where her friend's corpse had been. There was a bloodstain on the hardwood floor within the borders of the outline. The sight of the bloodstain made a garbled choking noise come from Leah's throat. She ran into the kitchen, bowed her head over the sink, and vomited up the orange juice she'd had for breakfast.

Pietro stood next to her and watched as she turned on the faucet to wash the vomit down the drain. She averted her eyes: tears were blurring her vision.

"I'm sorry; I had to do this." His voice was gentle.

"Yeah."

"Would you like to sit down?"

She went to the kitchen table and took a chair. The detective seated himself across from her.

"Can you handle a question right now?"

"I guess so."

"Was Miss MacIntyre a little crazy?"

"No, not at all."

"We found a ring in the vegetable drawer of her refrigerator. It seems an odd place to keep jewelry."

"I can't imagine why she'd do that. Can I see it?"

"Sure. We already checked it for fingerprints and there's none except the victim's." Pietro went to the refrigerator and pulled out a wad of crumpled brown paper stained with juice. "It was buried under a bunch of vegetables, and the tomatoes leaked on it." He handed the wad to Leah.

She unwrapped the multiple layers of brown paper and found a small black-leather ring box. Opening it, she saw a white-metal ring bearing a pinkish-violet oval stone about one inch wide and more than an inch long. "It's an amethyst."

"Is it valuable?"

"No, not with that pale color. I have some amethyst jewelry. Value is based on color, not size. Most of my stones are much darker than this one and they still didn't cost too much. My most expensive piece only cost about $100. This ring is pretty, if you like gaudy stuff, but it's not worth much."

"The fact that she put in her vegetable drawer makes me think she didn't care much about it."

"It must've gotten in there by mistake. Maybe she had too much wine one night and got confused; I don't know." She put the ring on one finger and looked at it.

"It is pretty gaudy."

Leah didn't answer. When she slipped the ring on, she felt the strangest sensation; as if there was a powerful magnetic current between her flesh and the bauble that made the two want to be together. The ring felt like a part of her now. She didn't want to take it off; she couldn't take it off.

She took a deep breath. "I . . . I'd like to keep this. I know it's too early to be claiming any of my inheritance, but, well, this ring feels like a bit of Emma. Could I take it home with me?"

"This is the scene of an ongoing investigation—you can't be carrying stuff out of here."

"Please." Leah put her hand to her chest, pressing the ring close to her heart.

"I could get in a lot of trouble if I let you have that."

"Please; it's important to me." Tears began to fill her eyes and roll down her cheeks.

"Don't start crying again! Take the ring and go. I'll know where it is if we need to get it back from you."

"Thank you, thank you!"

"I must be an idiot," Pietro muttered.

Leah grabbed the ring box and wad of paper, and ran out the door.

 # Chapter 2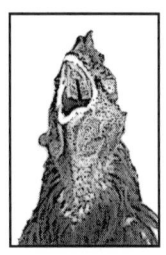

TUESDAY

Leah tended to her animals per her usual morning routine and sat at the kitchen table. As she ate her breakfast cereal, she thought about the vineyard behind her property and the way it offered perfect cover for a two-legged predator. Since she knew of no one who had a personal desire to see Emma dead, she'd concluded it was a thief who'd chosen the house at random and broke in hoping to find valuable loot. It was possible the person could return to the area and decide to invade her home.

The Destroyer jumped up onto the kitchen table and pointed his nose at his destination: Leah's bowl of cereal. "No, Malcolm! Milk's not good for you." She rose from her chair and pushed him to the far end of the table as he squealed in protest.

The cat stayed where his owner had put him as she went to a kitchen drawer and pulled out a phone book. She opened the yellow pages to the security-system installers and began to read ads as she finished off her cereal. "I like the looks of this one," she said to Malcolm, and went to her office to check reviews of the business that were posted online.

No one hated this particular establishment, so she went back to the kitchen and picked up the phone. A brief conversation indicated she could get what she wanted: window and door sensors for the house, covert outdoor night-vision surveillance cameras with audio for the front and back of her dwelling—including the front of the backyard shed that served as her exercise room—and live feeds that would upload to her computer and the cloud. They would do the work tomorrow and have it finished by the end of the day.

"Let's get to work, Malcolm." She went to her office and woke up the computer. The cat settled down in front of the monitor and watched the screen as she opened her graphics application and resumed work on the bank's ad. If she pushed herself, she could have it finished in time to make it to her evening jitterbug class.

Leah went into her bedroom, followed by the ever-attentive Malcolm, and began to change into comfortable dancing clothes: baggy pants, a T-shirt, and flat leather shoes. She considered the giant stone on her finger and decided she could survive taking it off, as it would get in the way while holding hands with a dance partner.

She went into the kitchen and pulled the wad of brown paper from a drawer. The leather box was inside it, and she opened it and put the ring back in its container. As she began to wrap the multiple layers of paper around the box again, she noticed two of the layers were adhering to one another; stuck together with the dried tomato juice that had leaked onto them.

She pulled the two layers apart and found between them a folded piece of yellow paper. She unfolded it and saw it was a receipt from a jewelry store's appraiser. Reading it, she learned Emma had submitted the ring for an insurance-coverage appraisal but then cancelled the process the same day: the day before her murder.

"Well," Leah said to the cat, "I guess she changed her mind when she realized the appraisal would cost more than the ring's worth." She put the box back into the wad of paper and stuffed it in the drawer.

★

WEDNESDAY MORNING

The security-system installers showed up early. Leah had hoped to begin work on a design for an album cover starting first thing in the morning, but found she couldn't concentrate with a bunch of strange men stomping about and shouting at one another.

She sat on the couch and glared out a front window. She'd been there only a few minutes before she saw the Citröen pull up and park in front of her house.

She went to the door and opened it. Lieutenant Pietro was coming up the front path; a large basset hound plodding along at his side. "Good morning, Miss."

"Lieutenant."

"Do you mind if I bring my dog inside? He won't hurt your cats; I promise."

"They're all hiding, anyway. Come on in." The detective and his dog entered. "I thought the basset hound was a nonexistent part of your Columbo act."

"Oh, no! He's my buddy. I had to bring him along with me today 'cause my wife's out of town and he doesn't like being alone." Pietro smiled. "I see you're having a security system installed."

"Yes."

"What features are you getting?"

"The works. The only thing missing is a system of land mines along my backyard fence. They didn't think it was very funny when I asked for that."

"Are you getting a surveillance camera in the back? If your friend had put one of those in place, it would've made my job easier."

"I'll show you." She led the man and his dog into the backyard. "They're putting one right there by my kitchen window, and there'll be another one at the front of that shed."

"What's in the shed?"

"Exercise equipment. I have to stay in shape for my dance classes. Doing the jitterbug proper ain't easy."

"How often do you have classes?"

"Twice a week. I went last night, but I couldn't dance; I had to leave. You have to have feelings to dance, and I don't seem to have any emotions right now, aside from irritability. I don't know if irritability is really an emotion, but I suppose it is."

"Maybe you're suffering from a state of high-functioning shock. No feelings right now might be a good thing." Pietro looked down at his canine companion. "Do you mind if I let my dog off his leash?"

"I don't want him to get hurt."

"What could hurt him here?"

"Chicken Little."

"Your chicken?"

"The last time I let a dog go loose in this yard, he decided to check her out and she nailed him hard in the nose with her beak. He yelped and ran into the house."

"Must've been a small dog."

"It was a full-grown German shepherd."

"That story is hard to believe."

"Have I lied to you yet?"

"Your explanation for the appearances of your image on the videos isn't credible."

"All right, then! Turn him loose and see what happens!"

The detective bent down and unclipped the leash from the dog's collar. The hound stepped forward to do what hounds do best; putting his nose to the ground in an olfactory investigation of the property.

It didn't take him long to catch the scent of the chicken. Leah and Pietro stayed with the dog as he followed the trail leading to the bird. She was scratching in the dirt, pecking at bugs in the ground, and minding her own business till the hound drew near enough to present a threat to her.

She raised her head and looked the dog in the eye. He shuffled forward; his facial expression showing as much fascination as the inscrutable basset visage can muster. Closer and closer he moved, till his nose was a foot from hers.

Her red wings flapping, the hen leapt forward and nailed him right between the nostrils with her beak. The hound let out a brief howling cry, tossed his head in pain, and trotted to the safety of his master's side.

"I'll be damned."

"I told you! Now your dog got hurt because you wouldn't believe me! You better apologize to him!"

He stroked the hound's head. "And you're worried about her being eaten by the local wildlife at night?"

"There's a big difference between a hungry coyote and a well-fed domesticated dog."

"I suppose there is."

"I'm getting really tired of you not believing what I say. It's rude!"

"It's my job."

"Yeah, I guess it is." Leah nodded. "How goes the investigation?"

"We questioned Miss MacIntyre's associates and employees; haven't learned anything useful yet. Her neighbors were all asleep at the time of the murder, so they didn't hear or see anything. The house hasn't yielded any leads, and we've hit a dead end tracing the murder weapon."

"I'm very sorry to hear that."

"Criminals make mistakes. We'll keep digging; something should come to light sooner or later."

"I hope so."

"If anything comes to your mind, you'll let me know; right?" He dug in his pockets and located a business card. "Anything comes up; you give me a call." Leah extended one hand to accept the card, and Pietro saw the ring. "You wear that all the time?"

"Yes."

"Doesn't it get in the way?"

"Only when I dance, and since I can't dance right now, well; there you are."

"I see." He clipped the leash onto his dog's collar. "Don't forget to give me a call if anything comes up."

"I won't."

FRIDAY AFTERNOON

Leah leaned back in her office chair and sighed with relief. She'd finished the preliminary plan for the album cover well before the deadline, which would make the music publisher happy. There was an order for three more covers to be worked on, but their deadlines were several days off and there was no rush.

She stared at her computer screen and considered the lack of progress made by the homicide detective. The absence of leads made her angry. She thought about the receipt for the cancelled ring appraisal. Emma had been to that jewelry store the day before she was killed. Maybe; just maybe; there was something to be learned from the person in the store who had spoken with her.

Leah walked into the shop and glanced at the glass cases holding displays of sparkling jewels and gleaming gold. Flashes of green fire drew her closer to one of the cases. She looked through its glass top and saw an emerald and platinum necklace.

A red-haired saleswoman in a severe black dress stood behind one row of cases. The young lady wore a suspicious look on her heavily made-up face as she stared at the visitor, who was dressed in her usual outfit of sweats and sneakers. Leah had an urge to shout, 'Yeah; I'm no trophy wife!' but kept her mouth shut. She put her hands out onto the top of the glass case as she studied the glittering emerald necklace. The overhead lighting in the store was designed to make the most of the jewels on display and made the big stone on her finger sparkle.

A man came from a back room behind the counter and approached her. His head was shaved, and he had a broad, flat, puffy face mounted on a neck much thicker than his bare skull. His body was heavy-set, with a muscular build augmented by fat, and his black suit didn't fit him well. Except for the suit, he looked like a walking mug-shot of a thug. "Can I help you?"

"Yes, thank you. I'm looking for the appraiser."

"That would be me." He smiled.

Leah pulled the receipt from her sweat-pant pocket. "Do you remember this?"

He examined the piece of paper. "I'm sorry. I don't recall this transaction."

"It was regarding this ring." Leah raised her hand so the man could get a closer look.

"I don't recall seeing that piece before. It's, ah; different, isn't it?"

"Are you the only appraiser working in this store?"

"Yes. Could I get a closer look at your ring?"

"Sure." She removed the bauble and handed it to him.

He looked at the stone for a moment before returning his attention to the receipt. "Emma MacIntyre, it says. Is she a friend of yours?"

"Yes."

"It's a shame she changed her mind about the appraisal. It's a unique ring; I'd like to spend some time with it. It's very interesting."

"I suppose so. To me, it's just an oversized amethyst, though it has a lot of sentimental value for me."

"Yes." The man pulled a pad out from a drawer. "I'd be happy to do an appraisal for you."

"No, thanks."

"It's an interesting ring; really, it is. I'll do an appraisal for you for fifty dollars."

"No, thanks."

"How about ten dollars?"

"No."

"The offer stands. I'll write down this price for you, and you can come back if you change your mind." He wrote a few words on the receipt pad. "Could I have your name and address, please?"

"Could I have my ring back?"

The man laughed. "Of course." He returned the ring and bent over his pad again. "Name and address, please."

"No, thanks." She turned and walked out.

Her old sedan was parked in front of the store. She settled into the driver's seat and dug around in the beat-up brown-leather handbag she'd bought at the Salvation Army. Finding her phone and Pietro's business card, she entered his cell number and heard him answer.

"Lieutenant . . . this is Leah Thorsen."

"Yes."

"You said I should call if anything came to mind."

"Yes."

"Well, I've got something in my mind now. I found a receipt with that ring. Emma took it to an appraiser the day before she was killed. I just went to see him so maybe; maybe I could learn something."

"What was it appraised for?"

"Insurance."

"No, I mean the value."

"She cancelled the appraisal before it was done."

"I see."

"Anyway, I went in and asked the guy . . ."

"What guy?"

"The appraiser."

"Okay."

"I asked him if he remembered anything about her going in with the ring, and he said he didn't."

"So?"

"He was really, really interested in the ring. He even offered to do an appraisal for me for ten dollars!"

"You're surprised by that price?"

"Yes, it's insanely low. And the other thing is . . . if he's so fascinated by this ring, why doesn't he remember seeing it only seven days ago?"

"I suppose he sees a lot of customers. He can't remember everyone who comes into the store."

"Something's wrong here!"

"I don't see that."

"Ten dollars for an appraisal doesn't strike you as a bit strange?"

"What do you want me to do about it?"

"Question him!"

"He already told you he doesn't remember the victim going into the store. He'd tell me the same thing."

"Haul him in and interrogate him!"

"Because he gave you a low price for an appraisal of an inexpensive ring?"

"Something's wrong with him!"

"I'm sorry. There's nothing I can do."

"I see. I'll let you go, then."

"Okay."

"Just one more thing . . ."

"Yes?"

"You're no Columbo!" She turned off the phone and dropped it into her purse. The thought crossed her mind that he'd been nice to her most of the time and she shouldn't have insulted him like that, but her anger and frustration took precedence over fairness.

Leah started the engine, turned to look around the car in preparation for getting out of the parallel-parking space, and saw the appraiser standing in front of the store smoking a cigarette. Their eyes met, and he gave her a smile and a wave goodbye.

"Creep!" She hoped he could read her lips.

★

SATURDAY

Mrs. MacIntyre walked barefoot over the marble floor. Three hundred years of human steps had polished the tiles to a fine smoothness. Tightening the belt of her heavy silk robe, she went through an open doorway and out onto the main balcony of the palazzo. The lights in the garden were on, and lent a lovely glow to the jets of water splashing in a circle around the larger than life-size statue of a winged goddess that stood in the center of the grand fountain below.

"Are you coming to bed, dear?" said a voice from within the room.

She wiped the tears from her eyes. "Not yet, John."

"I'll see you in a bit, then." The silver-haired gentleman turned away and vanished through a gilded archway.

Leah was fussing over the letter spacing for the title of an album cover when the phone next to her computer rang. She picked it up. "Hello."

"Is this Leah?"

"Yes."

"I'm Mrs. MacIntyre. I'm Emma's mother."

"Oh! I'm so glad to hear from you! I wanted to call you, but I don't have your number; I don't even know where you live."

"We're not at home. We're at our place outside Florence."

"Firenze? What time is it there?"

"Midnight. I didn't think I could fall asleep, so . . . I thought I'd call my daughter's best friend. She gave me your number a long; a long time ago."

"I'm so sorry, Mrs. MacIntyre. Emma was a wonderful person. She was so kind, and so smart; just wonderful."

"Yes, she was. We were proud of her. She could've lived a very easy life; we would've given her a comfortable income, but she wanted to earn a living with her engineering talents."

"Yes. She enjoyed her work. She was a truly happy person."

"Was she really happy?"

"Oh, yes! She loved running her business."

"I spoke with her a few days before; before she went, and she told me she was happy, but it's comforting to have you confirm it."

"It's my pleasure."

"There won't be any services. She didn't want a funeral."

"Okay."

"She told me some time ago that she planned to leave everything to you."

"I feel, well, uneasy about that. You're her family; she should've taken care of you."

"Oh, my dear; we don't need caring for."

"But . . . it doesn't seem right. Why leave everything to me?"

"I know why. Emma told me you're an artist."

"Yes, I am."

"She said you're quite talented, but you have to earn a living doing commercial work." The way the lady said 'commercial' indicated she held a severe distaste for the meaning of that word. "She wanted you to be free to explore your talent."

"That's so kind of her."

"Just promise me you will be very careful with the Jubilee Star."

"Jubilee Star? What's that?"

"The pink diamond, of course."

Leah looked down at the ring on her finger. The emotional numbness she'd felt since finding her friend's corpse blossomed now into a feeling of total physical anesthesia.

"Are you still there, Leah?"

"Uh . . ."

"Are you all right?"

"Uh . . ."

"What's wrong?"

"Uh . . ."

"Leah! Speak to me!"

"Uh . . . hold on!" She sucked in a big gulp of air, then let it out slowly. That felt better. "You mean this huge thing on my finger isn't an amethyst?"

"Amethyst? God, no!"

"Oh."

"You're wearing it, then? She already gave it to you?"

"No. It's a long story."

"You shouldn't be wearing it without at least four armed guards surrounding you. Emma always kept it in a safety deposit box at the bank."

"She had it in her vegetable crisper. I thought it was just an; an ordinary ring."

"No, it's not ordinary."

"Do you have any idea why it was in the fridge?"

"Emma was in the habit of using it as a hiding place. Our cook used to find some very peculiar things in the refrigerator when she was a child."

"I guess she'd taken it out of the safe deposit box to get it appraised?"

"I suggested she get it appraised again the last time we spoke to each other. She had it insured for only thirty-million, and the value's gone up."

"Only thirty-million? Only?"

"Yes. A pink diamond of the same quality and size sold about a year ago for eighty-three million."

"There's eighty-million dollars on my finger." Leah's hands began to shake.

"You need to get that into a safety deposit box."

She looked at her computer's clock. "It's three o'clock. The banks close at two on Saturday. I can't get it in there until Monday morning."

"Then take it off and put it in the refrigerator, if you don't have a safe in your house."

"I don't. This is scary."

"Don't be afraid. No one but you knows it's a diamond, right?"

"The appraiser saw it."

"What appraiser?"

"I found a receipt with the ring. Emma had taken it to a jewelry shop for an appraisal but cancelled it before it was done."

"I told her not to do that! I offered to help her locate a competent appraiser in San Francisco, but she said she'd find one on her own. She wouldn't listen to me. She had no head for anything but engineering. The world of fine gems? She didn't know how to navigate it."

"I went into the jewelry store to see if I could find out anything about . . . well; she went in there the day before she was . . . the day before she left us. I wanted to see if the appraiser could tell me anything. He saw me wearing the ring."

"That's not good."

"He doesn't know my name, or where I live, so maybe it's not a problem."

"I hope so."

"I . . ." Leah paused.

"Yes?"

"I suspect this ring was given to Emma by you; right?"

"Yes. It was her eighteenth-birthday gift. It was given to me on my eighteenth birthday by my mother. If Emma had a daughter, she would've received it on her eighteenth birthday."

"This is a family heirloom. I shouldn't keep it; it's yours."

"I won't disregard my daughter's wishes. That would be disrespectful to her memory."

"It's eighty-million dollars."

"We don't need the money."

"You don't need eighty-million dollars?"

"That's correct."

"I don't know what to think about that."

"I live in a world quite different from yours. I assure you, while I do consider that amount of money to be significant, it's not worth disregarding Emma's will. And as family heirlooms go, I have many, and that stone is by no means the most precious one, from my point of view. If we were discussing a Rembrandt, things might be different, but when all is said and done, what you have on your finger right now is nothing more than a well-cut rock. It's not a masterpiece by any means; just a way of storing wealth in one small area."

"Okay."

"It's late, and I'm getting tired. Promise me you'll be careful so I can get a good night's sleep, yes?"

"Yes. Good night."

"Buona notte."

Leah hung up the phone and stared at the giant gem on her finger. She couldn't understand why anyone in their right mind would pay eighty-three million for a rock.

She went into the kitchen and opened the refrigerator door. The vegetable crisper didn't seem like such a great hiding place. Opening the freezer compartment, she withdrew a carton of strawberry ice cream. She grabbed a spoon from a drawer, dug into the top layers of the frozen dessert, jammed the ring down into the ice cream, smoothed it over with the spoon, and put the carton back in the freezer.

She took a seat at her kitchen table. Having such a valuable object in her refrigerator felt to her about as relaxing as having a gallon jug of nitroglycerin stored next to the burning flame of her water heater's pilot light.

Leah went to the cabinet over her sink and extracted a bottle of akvavit. Removing the top, she swallowed a long guzzle of the Norwegian liquor, then put the bottle back in the cabinet.

She sat down again, and Malcolm jumped up onto the table next to her. "Hey, handsome." She stroked his back while he purred and wiggled with pleasure. "Let's get back to work, boy. If I sit here thinking about that thing in the fridge, I'll lose my mind." Heading down the hallway to the office, the pair came to Leah's bedroom, and she stopped at the door. "Hang on, baby. I'm gonna indulge in a bit of superstitious activity."

She went to a wooden jewelry box that sat atop her bureau and opened it. Pulling out a necklace, she put it around her neck. Suspended from a heavy chain was a traditional *Sølje* pendant made of bronze; its oval shape adorned with curving linear forms. Leah's ancestors believed the spoon-like bits dangling from the bottom of the pendant protected the wearer against evil; most especially trolls. "It's an anti-troll necklace, Malcolm. This ought to keep us safe."

The pair returned to the office, and she resumed the adjusting of the letter spacing for the album's type.

★

Leah glanced out an office window. The sky was overcast; rain might be on the way. She decided to bring Chicken Little inside a bit earlier than usual so the hen wouldn't get wet.

She stepped out into the yard. "Chicken Little!" she called out. The woman didn't know if the bird recognized her own name, but the sound of her owner's voice usually brought the feathered creature forth.

She waited a few seconds, but the hen didn't show, so she went around the back of the shed to see if she was there. Nope; no bird.

Leah walked back towards the front of the building, intending to see if her pet was in the side yard. As she went around the corner of the shed, she almost collided with a man standing before its closed front door.

It was the appraiser. He wore khaki pants, a bulky dark-blue padded jacket, brown-suede hiking boots, black leather gloves, and held a gun in his right hand.

He raised the pistol and pointed it at Leah's heart. "Hello, Ms. Thorsen."

'Show no fear, don't move, and be yourself,' an ancestral voice within her whispered. "How did you get my name?" She kept her voice calm and even.

"I got your license-plate number."

"And you went online and paid for my personal information. How nice."

"I love the Internet!" He smiled.

"Right this second, I think it sucks."

"You don't seem very surprised to see me."

"I don't know . . . I wasn't really expecting you, but now that you're here, I'm not surprised at all."

"Then you know why I'm here?"

"Yes, I do."

"Let's get right to business, then. Give me the ring."

"You mean the diamond."

"Yes."

"No."

"What?" The left side of the man's face began to twitch; the corner of his upper lip darting skyward as his eye blinked in a rapid and synchronized rhythm matching the movements of the side of his mouth. "What do you mean, 'no'? Do you want to end up like your friend?"

"Not particularly."

"Then give me the diamond."

"Tell you what: I'll give you the diamond after you tell me the story of what happened between you and Emma."

"I'm in something of a rush. Give me the diamond right now, or I'll have to kill you."

"If you kill me, you'll never get the diamond. I've hidden it very well. Take the sure thing: tell me the story, and you get the rock. Don't tell me the story, and you'll have another murder on your hands with no diamond. Which do you prefer?"

He considered this proposal for a few seconds. "All right; I'll take the sure thing." His twitch subsided; becoming barely perceptible.

"Begin with Emma's trip to your store."

"It's not my store."

"I could tell that from the cut of your suit." Leah couldn't resist a tiny jab at the man's ego. "Let's start again: begin with her trip to the store where you work."

"She came in for an insurance appraisal."

"I already know that. Why did she cancel it?"

"I'm not sure. I wrote out most of the receipt and was about to put down the price . . ."

"What were you going to charge her?"

"A hundred and fifty."

"Okay; please continue."

"I, uh, I asked her for verbal confirmation of the appraisal fee before I wrote it down, and she gave me this look all of a sudden. I don't know what her problem was, but she demanded that I give her the unfinished receipt, and when I did, she snatched it from me and walked out."

"So . . . you memorized her address?"

"No, I had a copy on the receipt pad. She didn't see that it was a duplicating pad, I guess. She seemed in a rush to get out of the store."

"She must've realized she'd gone to the wrong appraiser."

"What do you mean by that?"

"I'm no expert on precious gems, but if I wanted an appraisal on a diamond worth a large fortune, I wouldn't go to somebody like you. I mean, are you really qualified to handle something like that? Besides, you reek of bad vibes, and you're a bit of a troll." The aforementioned ancestral voice had encouraged her to be herself, and she was going for it.

"You better watch what you say to me! I'm armed, and you're not."

"Would being polite to you change the end result of this encounter? I think not! Anyway, I've got the diamond, so you don't have all the power here."

He glared at her with an expression of unmitigated hatred as his broad, chubby face grew pink.

"What happened when you got to Emma's house the next morning?"

He licked his lips; looking like he wanted to bite somebody. "Not much; I was only there for a minute."

"Not much happened? How can you say that?"

"Well, I didn't get what I came for; it was a waste of my time; just a great big waste!" The side of his face resumed its demented twitch-dance.

"Please be more specific. Give me every detail, and start at the beginning." Leah had a feeling the man wanted to share the story of his adventure and would enjoy being able to tell his tale.

"I parked on Starlight Road and went through the pasture next to her backyard and climbed through the barbed-wire fence and went to her house," the man was rattling off his story in a fast stream, "and broke one of the glass doors so I could unlock the other one. I opened the door and went inside, and she came running into the dining room in her nightgown. I told her to give me the diamond and she yelled, 'Go to hell!' at me. I shot her in the heart, and down she went! I was about to start lookin' for the diamond when I heard somebody poundin' on the front door and ringin' the bell. I figgered somebody heard the gun fire, so I ran for it. It mighta been a neighbor with a shotgun."

"How do you plan to get rid of the diamond once I give it to you? Who's going to pay for such a rare piece of stolen property?"

"Oh, there's always someone willing to pay."

"Who?"

"I . . . wait a minute. I told you everything you said you wanted to know. It's time to give me the diamond!"

"No."

"What do you mean, 'no'?"

"No, I'm not giving you the diamond."

"You promised!"

"I lied."

"I'll kill you if you don't give it to me!"

"You'll kill me if I do give it to you. Why should I give you what you want if you're just gonna kill me anyway?" Leah stared into the troll's ugly eyes and felt nothing; absolutely nothing. This nothingness might seem odd to some, but some folk who've stared down a gun-pointing thug know that feeling and therefore showing nothing can be the key to survival, and such an instinctive reaction isn't all that unusual for people of a certain type.

"Why in the hell aren't you scared?" The troll's eyes were beginning to bulge from their sockets in an almost freakish way. "What's wrong with you?"

"I'm not afraid of death," Leah replied. "It's a Viking thing."

The man began to shake, and his round, beefy face grew red. He stepped forward and pushed the pistol against Leah, right over her heart, and opened his mouth to speak.

"Buck**OW**!" Chicken Little announced herself with a loud hen-cry and thrust her beak like a tiny harpoon into the plump calf of the two-legged bad-vibe whale. He turned in the bird's direction with his arm out, aiming the pistol at empty air. A round black shape came down over his head, and he collapsed onto the ground.

The vardøger stood there with a broad grin on her face and Emma's cast-iron wok in her hands.

The double seated herself atop the unconscious man's stomach with her feet on either side of his head; the wok still held in both hands. "I have to call 911!" Leah said. The mute twin shook her head back and forth, and made various gestures which led Leah to believe that 911 had already been called.

She heard the sound of a distant siren; soon many sirens were screaming in a discordant chorus. She looked at the fallen man's face: he was coming out of his stunned state. "Stay right there, troll!" she shouted at him, "or my twin here will bash in your head with that wok!" The gun had fallen from his hand onto the ground. She didn't want to touch the weapon and interfere with any fingerprints that might be on it, so chose not to restrain him at gunpoint.

An officer, gun drawn, came into the yard through the kitchen door. "Don't move!" he shouted.

"His gun's on the ground!" Leah said. "We're unarmed!"

"Raise your hands!"

"You said not to move!"

"Hands up!"

The trio complied with the most recent command; the vardøger holding the two-handled pan in both hands as she raised them high into the air. "Drop the wok!" the officer yelled. The double broke into a huge smile, and the twelve-pound skillet fell onto the appraiser's chest. He choked out a loud grunt, but continued to hold his hands up.

Three more officers came through the kitchen door and charged into the yard; drawn guns pointed at the trio. "This is the man who killed Emma MacIntyre!" Leah wiggled the fingers of one raised hand in an attempt to point out the murderer without moving.

"Stay still!" The officers came closer to the trio; moving with caution.

"Get off him!" The first policeman watched as the vardøger stood up and stepped to one side of the man on the ground. "Sit down!" he told the ladies. "You two can lower your hands."

As the women seated themselves on the grassy earth, three of the officers stared down at the appraiser. They seemed content to leave him lying there with his hands in the air for the moment.

"What's going on?" one officer asked.

"He came into my yard with a gun and tried to rob me."

"Why is he lying on the ground?"

"My twin whacked him on the head with the wok and he fell down. She saved my life. He said he was going to kill me."

"That's what 911 told us. They heard what he said. Do you have a cordless landline on you somewhere?"

"No."

"How did the conversation get through to us?"

The vardøger sat there grinning, and pointed at her own chest.

"My twin's mute. I'm guessing she had something to do with it."

"Can I put my hands down now?" the troll asked.

"No!"

"Come on, Mike. He already got bashed twice with a cast-iron wok. Give him a break," an officer said.

"All right. Put your hands down, sir, but don't move."

"I got his confession on video, with audio," Leah said. "He was facing the camera the whole time. It was uploaded live to the cloud, so no one can say it was tampered with, right?"

"How'd you do that?"

Leah pointed to a small, inconspicuous grey box under the eaves of the shed. "That's a camera."

"Nice . . . it's practically invisible."

Lieutenant Pietro came into the yard. "What's going on?"

Leah pointed to the man on the ground. "That's the appraiser I told you about. He came into my yard with a gun, threatened to kill me, and tried to rob me. He confessed to killing Emma and gave all the details: details that only the police and killer would know. And there's the murder weapon." She pointed at the gun.

Pietro glanced at the vardøger, then bent down and looked at the pistol. "That looks to be the right caliber." He straightened up. "He confessed to who?"

"Me and my security camera."

"All right."

"I'm sorry I insulted you yesterday."

"Did you insult me?"

"Yes."

"Since I don't remember it, I'd say there's no need to apologize."

"Thanks."

Pietro addressed the youngest officer. "You men can Mirandize this guy, bag the gun, and get him out of here."

"What about the lady who creamed the guy with a wok?"

"What guy with a wok?"

"No, that lady there hit that man there over the head with that wok there. Do I need to bag the wok?"

"Why did she hit him with a wok?"

"He was threatening to kill her sister."

"Bag the wok and take the lady in for questioning."

"Good luck with that." Leah smiled for the first time in a week.

Chicken Little galloped through the yard and into the kitchen. The hen's movement caught Pietro's eye. "This place is a zoo."

"Four cats and a chicken do not constitute a zoo."

"I assume we can look at the video footage on your computer."

"Sure. Come with me."

Pietro went into the kitchen first. "Which way is your office?"

"Go through the door on your right."

He turned, took two steps forward, and a second later was flat on his back on the floor. "Are you all right?"

"I slipped on something."

"Here." Leah gave him a hand and helped him to his feet. "Sorry; Chicken Little poops when she's upset."

"I'm gonna need a chiropractor tomorrow."

"Sorry. I'll put her away before she does it again." The hen was waiting before the door to her safe place, and Leah opened it and let her go inside. "Just go straight down that hallway; my office is at the end of it."

When they entered the room, they saw the office phone was off the hook and lying in front of the computer. The feed from the security camera was playing out on the monitor, with the volume turned up to the maximum level. They could see and hear the officers in front of the shed taking care of business.

"Can you get this back to where the appraiser shows up in the yard?"

"Sure." It took a little while for Leah to figure out the new software. "I got it! Here he is."

"Lieutenant!" The young officer had entered the room.

"Yes?"

"I put that lady in my squad car and locked her in the back. I got into the driver's seat, and she was gone! She was locked in the back, and then she wasn't there! It's impossible! She's gone!" His voice was cracking a bit, and becoming shrill.

"Gone." Pietro gave a heavy sigh.

"What should I do?"

"Search the area."

"We did. She's gone."

"I really hate this."

"What should I do?"

"Forget about it."

Shaking his head, the officer departed. Pietro, standing behind the woman seated before the computer, let out another sigh. "I'm not saying a word, Lieutenant."

"You just did."

"Sorry."

"Go back to where you started, please."

They watched the video up to the point where Pietro arrived on the scene. "Can you burn this to a disc for me?"

"I think I can figure out how to do that. Give me a minute; this video stuff is new to me."

The detective took a chair and waited in silence as the woman carried out the task. When the disc was burned, she turned in her chair and looked at Pietro. "I'm just gonna say one thing."

"All right."

"In case you didn't notice, the sky is overcast, so no one was casting any shadows."

"I noticed."

"So, I guess no one can say this video lacks integrity."

"That's two things."

Leah handed the DVD to the man and waved her hand once in goodbye.

★

When the detective and officers were gone, Leah went about shutting the doors the men had left open. After closing up the kitchen and giving the hen her nightly cob of corn, she went to the front door of the house and examined it. Nothing was damaged, so it seemed the first officer on the scene hadn't forced it open to get inside. She assumed the vardøger had unlocked the bolts after setting up the communication between 911 and her computer.

She sat down at the kitchen table; completely drained. It was kind of strange: facing an armed killer and remaining calm throughout the entire exchange had been surprisingly easy . . . until it was all over. Now that the adrenalin rush was gone, she felt sucked dry.

Malcolm jumped up onto the table. "So, you've come out from under the bed. Good boy." He purred as she scratched him under his chin.

The sound of a kitchen cabinet being opened was heard by the woman and the cat. They turned their heads to see the vardøger taking the bottle of akvavit from the upper shelf. She took two shot glasses from another shelf and sat at the table across from Leah.

The vardøger filled the glasses, and the women held them up in a toast. "Skoal!"

Thank you for reading "Doppelgänger." As an independent author, I rely upon readers to spread the word about my work. If you enjoyed this story, please consider leaving a brief review on the book's page at Amazon.

Printed in Great Britain
by Amazon.co.uk, Ltd.,
Marston Gate.